INFINITE THOUGHTS

A collection of poems
By
Katlego M Masemola

ISBN: 978-0-7961-6580-0 (print)

978-0-7961-6547-3 (e-book)

Published by Fishermen JNK (Pty) Ltd

2941 Maphutha Mokoena Street, ga-Masemola, 1060

Limpopo, South Africa

The contents within this book are a work of fiction, names, characters, places, and incidents are either the product of the author's imagination or used fictitiously. Any resemblance to actual events, locales, or persons living or dead, is entirely coincidental.

For permission request please contact:

Email: fishermanats02@gmail.com

Contacts: +27 79 368 5346

Editor
Raymond Kgatuke

Acknowledgements

Nthabiseng 'Dimples' Choga
Raymond 'Commando' Kgatuke
Monoshi 'Miss Grey' Ledwaba
Michel K Lekala
Mpine Letlala
Dinga Makobe
Victor Mantati
Nthabiseng M Masemola
Kefentse Matea
Pontsho 'Mufasa' Rachuene
Mighty 'Jones' Ramushu
Brudance 'Neiloe' Rasehashi

Special thanks to the names above, the individuals whom stuck with me, read my nonsense until it made sense, it is with their feedback that this book is finally ready to face the world.

Table of contents.

Poem Page

1. Infinite thoughts

2. From afar

3. Captivated in chortles

4. A tip of my heart

5. Coke

6. Forbidden Flames

7. Jewels

8. Driven berserk

9. Poppy

_10._ Heroine

11. If I burn

12. Blood and sweat

13. Sweet children

14. Eighty

15. Rhotacism

16. Self-perplexity

17. Self-musing

18. Heightened Hopes

19. Presupposed

20. Sad sight!

21. Obstacles

22. Chinned Up

23. Early days

24. Hot or cold

25. Displacements

26. Miserable

27. Would you?

28. Living anyway

29. Toilet

30. Casualty

31. Oh sugar happens!

32. Cliché!

33. Unheard

34. Parasites

35. Mournful
36. Either way!
37. The boy knock kneed
38. A man gets tired
39. Graveyard
40. Rumour
41. Death Note
42. Death Came
43. Mahlale a ngwana
About the author

1. Infinite thoughts

Common flaw thinking we have enough time
Ergo we eat, release, sleep,
Read, sing and write some bad poetry.
Caught in the web of our own mystery.

Nothing about the world's existence makes sense
Except that it is there, or rather here... immense,
The quiddity of time for instance-
The one entity which never changes,
Yet enhances,
And for some enigmatic cause, we age.

Time keeps on rolling all the way to infinity
The one place it may never reach, potentially,
But what if we're on the infinite already?
Hence the endlessness cycle of life itself, steady and
heavy.

For some cause everything is balanced-
The concept of life and death, meat and teeth,
Love and hate, male and female,
Hunger, food and toilet, a perpetual tale,
And barriers, language and race.

They say God created everything

But where does God come from?
Did he or she... or it, just appear out of nowhere
And create a whole universe out of absolute nothing?

Who wrote the stories, who crafted the names?
Orange and green, brown and yellow,
The answering box remains empty and hollow
But more questions arise, a constant follow.

Who came up with Nina, Spear, Tsitso or Oklahoma?
Tlhatlhamedupi, Kgolomodumo, Bogobe, Propaganda,
Ntukuduku, Xikwembu... Mamma Mia!
Why does John rhyme with George?
Where do the other days go, who knows?
Who knows the beginning, as life flows?
What is life, what purpose are we serving?
Are we here to eat, release, sleep,
Read and reproduce and respond to any kind of stimuli,
In an endless dance until we die?

Truth is... or speculation
The system is rigged:
No mortal man knows even an ounce we've dug
Because we just came, and we are already going!

I cannot help but to fiddle with these infinite thoughts,
Ever flowing,
And drive myself to endless madness,
Unknowing...

When two entities are connected by love, together they lack anything – Katlego M Masemola

2. From afar

From afar I gazed
Fed eyes enough to amazed,
Desired to sing heart and mind.
From afar I gazed...
When near she came,
Arose impeccable opportunity to say hello
But inferno cuddled up inside
And outside I froze... still trying - to hello.
I grow fond of her everyday
Yet feel less of a man every time I sway,
I never shot my shot, eyed her in the eye
And told her my core - she makes me bling and fly...
It pains that I cowered,
Hid behind bad blague, overpowered,
In fear of rejection by treasured.
From afar I still gaze, disheartened and measured.

3. Captivated in chortles

I discern a nugatory void within
Festering like a neglected sin,
Nothing I do seems sufficient to occupy the vacant space
Which makes me wonder about whence has it been dug?
Unflaggingly following a long river of flinty cogitations,
An antidote flogged, it is her chuckles I miss.
The beautiful mug I met at sundown
Her giggles cast a spell I can't unseat.
I burned my soup brooding if she's fell fed.
Spend aeons reminiscing her laughter which is more elegant
It beats the songbird
Heard from relaxing deep within the forest.
The situation leaves me feeling like a child
Missing an uncle whose gifts beguile.
Her laughter lingers, sweet and pure,
Captivated in chortles, my heart's allure.

4. A tip of my heart

I am not one for words
So here goes a tip of my heart:
I like how it feels to be loved by you
I cannot contain myself when you are near
I see you
And I feel a rush of emotions all at once
I do not know which one is which
But it feels good that you make me tick.
I am not one for words
But I am yours out of these many billion souls.

5. Coke

So smooth and strong, strikes each core within,
Paralyses and mops the floor with me, a win.
A voice too pleasant, so addictive in its tone,
Can't go a second without it, I'm never free.
I am haunted by these whispers of delight,
Mesmerising tunes,
All to feel that harmonic heartbeat,
Sonic enchantment.
Has me hooked like I'm on coke and nuts.
A vocal treasure, poets refer to as sweet melodies.
I finally found it echoing in my ears
Igniting infatuations and quelling all my fears.
From my weak heart, rendering me helpless,
Overwhelmed with love, emotions so relentless,
Which amplifies feelings of bright futures.
Blooming in the softest light, happy dreams.

6. Forbidden Flames

It's wrong what we do, bad on so many levels,
You have yours, I have mine, the victims.
Yet here we are! In these tangles revels.
Here we are with flames within our souls, burning bright.
Here we are smuggling bits of ourselves, hiding from sight,
Behind closed doors and curtains, in the silent of night.
Here we are sneaking about like teenagers past curfew
Escorting that one beat of their fragile hearts, that ensue
Forbidden love, intense and true.
We do it anyway, for the thrill, and the feel
To love what's taboo, a dangerous deal,
For in the secrecy, our passions conceal.
Thoughts of you run wild, can't be controlled,
The urge to caress, a feeling so bold,
Overpowered by desire, our story unfolds behind a blind.
I want you anyway despite morals that fray.
Social constraints can't keep us away.
I-want-you anyway! Come what may.

7. Jewels

A gem shone bright from the front porch
Sat quietly and swiftly as it reflected its bosoms' torch.
A glimpse almost blinded my sight
But I am glad my eye was clutched tight.
What does it await? I ponder and stare,
Conjecturing with a river of glances, here and there.
What if it's a love trap cunningly laid?
A snare for the delicate, hearts mislaid...
But my attention already drools over, desire inflamed...
I am going to steal it, my heart untamed.
Make its heart sync with mine, a rhythmic dance.
To this day, the gem in my hands, a trance.
The gem is an egg, fragile and rare,
I will forever hold it with utmost care
For one mistake it shatters like glass
And all its treasures lost to the surface, a distant memory.
It is safe only in my benign embrace.
I'm Gollum, and it's my precious, my grace.
It is mine, and mine alone.
A treasure to cherish, a love of my own.

8. Driven berserk

I am losing my mind
Playing with thoughts of her, her eyes so kind,
How it feels when she touches my hand
With soft and tender fingers, a feeling so grand.
I am going insane
Visualising her smile, contagious and plain.
I am losing my senses
Reminiscing her soothing voice, breaking all defences.
I am bananas
Looking at her pictures, her poses so glamourous.
Her curvy body in a yellow dress,
Exposing bits of herself, a sight to impress.
I am officially bonkers
Now that she is here, my heart conquers.
Driven berserk, lips on mine
No clue how to curb this love so divine.
I am now a certified madman
At the park with a hand in pocket and a huge grin,
Lost in the madness of love's sweet sin.

9. Poppy

There it lays, my sleeping beaut
More gorgeous in its slumber, truth.
In its alluring grin, I hang imprisoned.
My eyes confined in beauty's vision.
As its aesthetic visage calmly channels grace,
A gulp of air, I gaze upon its face
Like a scorpion trapped in glass,
Inaudible I am, perched on a rocking chair.
Easy on the eye, I remain consumed and weak.
Is it dawn already, a dream's demise?
I realise I am leaving in my dream's disguise
As sunrise settles on its messed raven hair,
I beam solo, caught unaware,
Baffled by the hue of one's heart.
It is not love at first sight,
Nonetheless a leering event in the light.
Love, as sweet as it may be,
Is mysteriously inexplicable.

10. Heroine

You taught what it means to give in,
To trust and love will all my being.
I was fleeting, and you unmuted me,
Created my zone of comfort, set me free.
Reminded of the shade of my teeth,
You are the reason I shine out the darkness.
What more could I strive for?
You stepped in and I stopped whining.
The one at the mountain peak sees all,
Every time I tilt my pupils at you, I feel tall,
Like I'm on top of the world,
Seeing all that is and not, the clear, open air.
The rich desires more
The poor want what they lack
The greed want it all
And here I am
Wondering what I am to do,
Since I want all of you.
I am not greedy nor wealthy,
Yet I take my steps with pride, my head help high
Belly leading my way, for I have what breeds the peace,
It's priceless yet more precious, my worries cease.
I sleep like a baby knowing you're near

KATLEGO MASEMOLA

Knowing you have my six, my dear.

11. If I burn

No one chooses to fall in love,
The love no one understands
Hence the many writings thereof.
It picks us randomly, with playful hands.
I used to be happy, not extreme but at peace.
I was doing fine! Focused with a clear mind.
I thought my heartache would never cease,
No more dating, love left behind.
Who wants to feel pain, always cry?
Oppressed by heartache and sorrow's tide?
"I am never good enough", my constant sigh,
"Not handsome enough, broke", negative notions collide.
I had given away all hope for love.
"I am done!" I said to myself, so sure
until one descended from above,
And my eyes met hers, a heart so pure.
From just watching her walk down the park, so serene,
In tight blue jeans, and black sandals, ugly toes, no pretence,
Her gentle steps as if she did not want to hurt the lawn...
From then I knew I wasn't done yet, in her presence
For a moment my heart beat steadily,
As a rush washed over my body's frame,
I've never felt more alive, so readily

in my entire life, ignited by her name.
This is me "If I burn, I burn!"
Walking toward her, heart in a frenzy,
"If I die I die!" for her I yearn,
"If I burn, I burn! If I die, I die!" Intensely.

INFINITE THOUGHTS

Hope makes us willing to suffer –
Katlego M Masemola

12. Blood and sweat

Blood is spilled across the street
Scattered inside the walls, once a sweet home.
Blood drops deep from a heart in pain,
An agonising wound, a good heart slain.
The blood of a father. Hard-working and true,
Felled by laziness and greed, from his own blood too,
For early inheritance and insurance, they conspired.
A loving father, by kindred, expired.
The blood of a mother, caring and kind,
Mugged, molested, and left lifeless,
Confined by sons who grew right before her eyes.
A loving mother, in sorrow, lies.
The blood of an innocent child, pure
Left in the care of a trusted uncle,
A kid robbed of her infantile.
Innocence lost, in a trusted place.
The blood of a citizen, concerned and brave,
Accused of exercising right to freedom of speech
And not minding her own matters, she paid the price
A voice silenced.
The blood of a police man
Brutally murdered
By the very same he swore to protect and serve.

INFINITE THOUGHTS

A shield and protector fallen, in duty's sphere.
This is the blood of truth and hope
The blood of desperations, promises and commitments.
This is the blood of morale, and lost integrity, and regrets.
This blood is ours
Kin and kin
Our brothers and sisters.

13. Sweet children

Physically delicate, emotionally profound in baffling ways
Peace and joy they bring at this fragile age!
Only quiet and peaceful in their slumber's embrace,
More cute and lovely, yet mischief's trace.
Evil and innocent, both they may seem,
For them toddlers know not from reality's dream.
As guardians we fear on their behalf,
To what is fed and what they become, in life's draft.
Oceans sing aloud from the red horizons bright,
Curiosity fed as the sun set,
Hence they lend ears to the melodies, the world's call
Prepared to swallow them whole, temptations enthral.
Leading to their worst, acquainted with greed
In this ruthless life, only the strongest succeed.
Our sweet children! Is home forgotten? Left behind?
In our hearts, your safety we constantly mind.

14. Eighty

My days and I have grown old,
And the winter keeps growing strong.
The children I envy but I'm doomed
So long as the beard grows grey and long.
Summer remains my best season,
Early bird is the sunrise, warms my heart,
Blankets hug me tight, pyjamas close to clean
For my bed at dawn is free from night's depart.
Eighties and wrinkled, slow as snail marks my pace,
Pleasure's chance slim to none found,
A glare at young and warm magnets chaos, a fleeting chance,
A man only dreams on, and stare up the sky's blue profound.
If only age's grip can gently hold,
Perhaps days wouldn't feel so cold.

15. Rhotacism

The worst possible affliction to ever exist
Making its sufferers unable to persist and pronounce it.
My life is a joke, they all seem to find it amusing.
My sister Lerato, in laughter, uneasing.
Every time I call her name,
It's met with a smile, always the same.
I recall having to read in English class, the dread
And getting stuck on the word 'threw'
Then again on 'through', to failing every oral in Afrikaans class.
My words a maze, I can't get through.
I tutored past tenses in the fourth grade, I tried
Draw and its past tense kicked me out of the classroom.
My confidence pries, a struggle to cope,
Feeling lost without much hope.
My lover's name is Prudence, sweet,
But her name, my tongue can't greet
Never told her I love her in my native speech,
Nor called her by name even once, always out of reach.

16. Self-perplexity

Mama always speaks of grandkids' delight,
I stand on the other side, can't get it right.
I said to her, "Hello I am Katlego, you can call me kay!"
And I was politely asked to wipe the smirk away.
No matter what I do or say
Why can't I simply find my way?
They always tell, "Be yourself, be true".
I have been me since aeons, feeling blue.
I grab all opportunities in the blink of an eye
But somehow lose each one of them like whoosh! They fly.
This is actually sad. The feeling I can't shake,
Every chance, another mistake.
I cannot get the girls, nor master math
A bright future ahead, yet no clear path.
I wonder aimlessly without a destination,
Lost in a sea of self-perplexation.

17. Self-musing

Dear brain,
Why do you always let me down?
You turned a blind eye back in high school
And cost me my grades, thought he was a salesman
When he came to scam us, now we're broke
All because you let him dance on our plan.
Dear tongue,
My favourite organ, my delight
The middle man between my favourite dish and bite.
I cannot lie, I am disappointed in you
As you decided to jam on the spot, lips lost at sea.
Well now she is gone, along with my only chance.
Dear feet,
I know not what to say to you,
I had finally scored some seconds to dance with her,
Only to have you boot it all up,
I trusted you, counted on you, you were my only hope!
It is sad when the only hope kept stumbling on her feet.
Dear eyes,
If your task is to look out, how did you not see them coming?
The failures, embarrassments and heartbreaks,
Pain so deep, now self-esteem asleep.
Eluded by the bad that appeared good,

INFINITE THOUGHTS

My spirit broken, with none to trust.
If it's not the battle with the world, it's the war inside.
An evil rot, the immortal cancer that bullies my body around,
A scourge to my being! A plague that refuses to be eradicated.
I rest my case, you are champion!
Dear me,
Why this much hatred toward me?

18. Heightened Hopes

If only I wasn't short, I'd shoot my shot,
And score the best goal of all, hit the jackpot.
But no she regard me a five-two
And only tall she's attracted to.
Are there steroids for height to gain?
High heels for men, to ease the pain?
I'd do anything for her, it's true,
Except to reach top shelf is a pain anew.

19. Presupposed

I thought I had it, in the palms of my mitts.
I thought I had it, lost wits.
Benighted and reckless, my folly swept,
Stubbornness grasped tighter, I wept.
My very own stupidity swept it like smut,
Prevailed by stubborn to grasp tighter.
Credit to my hideous ways, I am just as dirt.
Broke Precious for I took gentle for harder.
Lurid memoirs clear, more vivid they stay
And vision as night to day, comes to brain,
But the new certitude pains more solid and rigid.
But men don't cry... She was never drawn!
Here I am trying to detox, but gone is gone.
I can use a drink but it's on its grounds I'm all alone.

20. Sad sight!

As I live and breathe!
I see things no child should see;
I see things no parent should conceive.
If only I was blind!
I wouldn't see a parent's distress
Laying a child to eternal rest.
A whole future fades on a tombstone,
All potential wasted to the graveyard, gone without trace.
All that could've been- could've been. Lost in time and space.
If only I was deaf!
I wouldn't hear the weeping of a widow
Lamenting for her fallen husband.
If only I was a tree!
Perhaps then I would be of use
Comfort those beneath me from life's abuse.
In the next life...
I wish to be a star so bright!
A glimmer of hope for all to see, shining through the night.

21. Obstacles

Up against the wall I stand,
Keen to find what lies behind,
Motivated by hunger's hand,
Driven by what I fondly mind.
Against the mountain I remain still,
The barrier to what I hold dear,
I stand firm through the mud before the hill
Pondering if all is worth the fear.
Wonders are fragile warriors, bold.
Life is a circle, lessons always unfold.
The wise are lions, stories told.
The brave never cease, hearts of gold.
I stealthily tackle my prey like a hunter
For he with sway is victor.

22. Chinned Up

He held his head up high
Through the gathering storm,
The clouds were darkening, days far from warm.
And his days were turning blue and blacker
Business bad, love divorcing
Drowning and chocking in debt, life enforcing.
His world fell apart as he bled from within.
Although his troubles hung on him like hair on soap
He still hung on and held his head up high
For he still had his mother, his only reason why.

INFINITE THOUGHTS

A smile which knows pain is more genuine than the rest –
Katlego M Masemola

23. Early days

Uncle told me to stand up to bullies' might.
First day at school, already nabbed a fist on sight
For grasping on tighter and tighter onto my lunch box.
The bully's deplorable look depicted a woe
And I only saw him as a foe.
As I live and breathe hardly at ease
With my sweaty palms wetting the floor
While immobile trying to forge bravery's mask
Yet failing miserably to covert fear's daunting task
Of the thought of what is to befall...
The bluffing brat is saved by the bell,
A reprieve from the imminent hell.
Caught stealing meat from the pot
Far over memories, four foot tall, slight,
Ten autumns old, meat handed at midnight
Clever junior quickly awayed to his bed.
Denied, and denied to the morn breakfast
To my alibi and witness was pillow and bed.
Papa was thrilled and proud
Mama was disappointed and mad.
The days missed by all men:
The Early days, our youthful den.
Now old and bearded,

INFINITE THOUGHTS

Dungeoned to society's expectations
And morals, and rules and regulations.
No matter how many times life transpires,
I will never forget my early days.
The days of comfort and simplicities.

24. Hot or cold

I like them hot
Except for the seasons.
They say summer is best
But it rains all the time
And when it don't, the shadows take a walk.
Scorpions we fear and crush in cold blood whenever
spotted,
A good snake is a dead one,
Insects you try dooming, but whom is really doomed?
All day and night we wear sweat and stink.
Bedrooms burning, too hot to sleep or think,
Clapping to songs mosquitoes sing
In our sleep, a constant ring.

Winter soldiers aren't we all?
It ripples through your clothes, a chilly thrall.
Blows all around, attacks from all sides,
Fingers freeze, noses sneeze, legs abide.
Body always caught in shiver's grip,
Away to sun, shadows slip.
Beanie on for ears,
In place, a sweater, and a hood, and a jacket.
Although it is as cold as heaven,

INFINITE THOUGHTS

At least four heavy blankets get you a goodnight.

25. Displacements

At what stares the blind
Never can they see.
Although something heard the sky they called exists,
Never how blue they will know.

Listens always the deaf
The sound of sound they will hear never.
Although words can see they
Can they read?

Their way eventually finds everyone
But the point will never get dumb and stupid
Enough clever they are because
Suffer on their behalf and we.

What saying am I really
Is that there are forces moving the universe
And around it, motions understand or know never can
we.
How do you think we always find our way?

Mysteries unseen, unheard,
Guiding forces in silence each day.

26. Miserable

Um... here goes nothing.
I am beginning to believe in God
And I think he hates me!
Am I naïve? Not a chance
Am I happy? Hmm... that's rich.

Every time I get an ounce of rejoice
The plane crashes, my heart broken in dozen pieces
again.
Call me mysterious loner guy,
But reasons! Loathing this life, I sigh.

The only thing I seem to enjoy is sleeping,
Dreaming no one cares what
But then the sun dawns awake in fright,
And reality becomes the nightmare.

It's hard having to adjust.
It's hard having to make unfits fit.
It's hard having to settle and accept
When you have no idea what is meant to be.

It's hard... to smile, chuckle and giggle
When neurons are on leave, no wiggle.

KATLEGO MASEMOLA

I must admit, screw denial.
I am crippled by this loss, no reason to beguile.

And um – miserable is my middle name.

Living in a never-ending game.

27. Would you?

Hold my hand, stay with me inside this chaos
Not let go no matter how hard it pains
Hold my hand for your sake
And I will hold yours, for mine. No breaks.

Hold my hand, hold it tighter,
Pull me closer, the world grows lighter.
Hold my hand in hardships dire,
Like you do in moments of complete sunny days we
admire.

28. Living anyway

They went to harvest honey from beehive,
Aware everything might take a dive,
They came happy but faces swelled and alive.
They stole Dawn and Vaseline
Went swimming where crocodiles preen,
Little they knew, danger unseen.
They went to fish in the dam's expanse
Hoping for a feast by chance,
Little they knew, rain would advance.
I went to speak to her for the first time;
Chinned up, grin checked, all charms in line.
Little I knew her boyfriend was boxing prime.
From the moment we are born,
From the moment we greet the morn,
We are doomed from the very beginning, yet not forlorn.
Death awaits with a grin so wide,
But we live, we dream, we bide,
We achieve, we don't... but we strive inside.

29. *Toilet*

Despised is a hard-working man,
Called names by community he well serves.
We away toddlers, fearing his span,
His filth and dirt, we think he deserves
Yet when troubled, we bolt to his side
For he unburdens off our heavy bundles
Without a single complaint, in him we confide,
He listens to our confessions like a priest on a sacred road.
Despised is a hard-working man.
The very same who wipes your seat, hand in hand.

30. Casualty

To stay I wanted but had to leave
Soldiers at war were dying, they began to grieve.
Military needed more men to fight,
Father insisted I go, proud in sight.
But soldiers were dying, they just said
No word said mother, only tears shed
And by dawn I was long gone.
Ninety six months, time moved on.
None of the boys returned,
Only a few man with medals for the families.
I hope father was proud,
War was won, but no feast nor crying, just quiet.
They say war is dying for your land
Some say it's making the enemy die for theirs,
I say war is quiet and peaceful
And boom! Utter chaos springs and screams
And pieces of peace and flesh swirl in the air with dust and blood
And pain and grief and hush in a split second.
Nonetheless none of it is worth,
Except I fell for my siblings' mirth.
I am a boy to man of no nation.
I am African, White, Indian, Asian.
I am just a fallen man
Who lost a life for a few metres of land.

31. Oh sugar happens!

The guitarist had a bad manicure,
Whole hand amputated, lost allure.
The rich man who recently wed
Was stabbed to pulp by his loving and kind wife yesterday.
The priest was shot dead in God's church
For not giving up the offering money, in the lurch.
The top athlete known world wide
Lost his legs to a car ride.
The ballet dancer tripped and fell on stage,
Stood up to face the music, but career in rage.
The soprano singer whose career just took flight
Was diagnosed with an oesophagus tumour, lost her light.
My neighbour who smoked his life away
Died from AIDS, not lung cancer's fray.
The village drunkard didn't die of a burnt liver
But of heart attack after staying sober for a week.

The motorist wasn't killed by her bike,
But a boomslang bite at a picnic's strike.
Positivity is the new Jesus, they say...
Life's ironies lead us astray.
Twtwts tltstw mdtbtb pieddyh etetdr errkeds-
Oh sugar happens, in life's threads!

32. Cliché!

Hope is a dangerous thing
It brutally scragged many of my lovely sisters.
She hoped the man she loved
Would stop beating her.
She could've left...
She hoped instead! That he'd change,
She hoped instead! That he'd stay true to his apologies.
She could've pressed charges
But he said, "I am deeply sorry my queen."
She could've left
But he swore, "I will never do it again".
She hoped! With blood flooding the bathroom floor.
She hoped! With tears flooding down her bruised cheeks.
She hoped! Wiping the mucus from her nose.
She hoped! Believing the man she loved loved her still
But bruises all over her body conveyed a different message.
She held on, hoping one day he'd stop
And he did stop, but with her broken and lifeless.
"Ye of little faith" they say to me
But I say
Hope is a dangerous thing
It brutally scragged many of my lovely sisters.

INFINITE THOUGHTS

Unlike being stupid, being in the dark is somewhat nice –
Katlego M Masemola

33. Unheard

Been stumbling in the dark
For far too long,
The edges begin to fray
I am hanging by a thread, barely strong.
And there's only one remedy.
Or there used to be...
I am a drop in the sea, floating free,
A grain in rice,
I am a thread on a sock
And on my last breath.
A dog with nothing but a bone and a bark
A wolf with only a howl
Which never reaches the moon
My notion means nil
And yet... with my last breath:
Dear God
It is I
They toy you hate the most,
Take me too
Like you did with my rest.

34. Parasites

The existence of enemies makes zero sense!
How can one shovel beneath such pretence?
How can one incarnate just to incarcerate
And block dreams you strive to create?
Are you ready for the Devil's deceit?
The one cloaked behind kinship, with motives discreet,
Driven by envy, dissatisfaction and spite,
Or perhaps dislike, hiding in plain sight?
Are you ready for closest phonies to betray?
At the apex of your triumph, they prey,
Like poison in your favourite meal, they lie,
Are you ready for the Devil nearby?

35. Mournful

I never wanted mother to leave, but leave she did.
In Heaven, they said, she found her place, her bid.
Couldn't Heaven had to take a chill? I wonder still,
It took her like its possession, against my will.
God needed her more, so they always say,
But I only had her ten short years, my dismay.
While He claims her for eternity, so divine,
In His kingdom above, where angels entwine.
Is it safe to say the Most High, with glory and might...
Is possessive, self-centred, in His Heavenly light?
Or is my grief that colours this view
Yearning for mother in skies blue and bright?
Each tear that falls, a testament to my pain,
A bond so profound, yet Heaven's gain.
In memories she lingers, a gentle guide,
Though in Heaven she dwells, always by my side.

36. Either way!

Life goes on, a very easy...
A very quiet – something,
I don't know
Life goes on either way.
Shift happens, it's agonising, unbearable
Beyond elucidation
But ordeal for just one to feel for another
Though far from being at one page.
An entity ceases to be,
A life of a daughter, a mother, a sister... a friend.
A dog, cat, a horse... a friend.
Either way it all ends at an unspecified point
And life just... goes on.
It's agonising, unbearable
Beyond healing,
A break would do - a timeout:
Take a minute, and gasp
But nothing awaits as you lament.
The relentless passage of time just keeps on passing,
The seconds ne'er stop running,
Life goes on either way
It doesn't heed anent you
But a life does, mine.

37. The boy knock kneed

I never knew his name!
His head was a travel bag, full of weight,
His neck couldn't carry its load
But his shoulder took it head on, straight,
He faced up always, knees kissed.
I was a grade above him, just a glance,
Only saw him during lunch break's chance.
He always seemed tired, always moaning.
He was a tortoise, couldn't run, always slowing.
One day when the bell rang, caught in the stair's centre,
Dropped a yellow pencil as he was bumped

Side to side by his hyper classmates.
They ran him over, and over, and over, and over,
Until silence fell, no sound usurped.

His teacher stood by the door, arms folded
Watched him slowly bend to pick his pencil.
I sat twenty metres from his three o'clock watching in
silence
Forgetting I had a noise making class to join
As he patiently stepped on the stairs like a snail.

Two days later on my way to school,

INFINITE THOUGHTS

He instantly died from a hit and run, cruel.
The road and his sister's uniform were drenched in his
blood.
I never knew his name!
Only observed from the sidelines, stood.
I never was his friend, though I was almost six,
I still remember the boy, knock kneed.

38. A man gets tired

A man gets tired!
A man gets tired of all the wrong and good he does.
A man breathes and bleeds, inside and out.
A man faces life's toll, without a doubt.
A man gets tired of a wife who won't submit,
A man gets tired of working tirelessly, enduring every bit,
For disobedient and disrespectful kin,
A man drowns in his own thoughts, feeling thin.
A man gets tired of fighting his demons day by day.
Crying inside, hiding the pain away.
Though deep down, he needs aid
Mending his wounds, keeping fears at bay.
A man gets tired of vile surroundings.
A man gets tired of his own difficulties,
A man gets tired... but he must keep on.
A man rests only in his coffin, when he is gone.

39. Graveyard

A place where all beds
Swallows up all men and its kindred
Flesh, skills and talents decompose within,
Lost dreams, scored goals, regrets.

It matters not if you were vegetarian
It matters not if you drank only milk and water
It matters not whether you went to church
Your space remains reserved until your bedtime charter.

What you did with your time,
What you did not,
Your preferences, wishes for and of the world,
It all ends six feet under, with you wrought.

A man goes all out for the bread.
A man leaves his everything for the graveyard's stead.

40. Rumour

A virus resides within our tongues and ears
The talks in the taverns
The say with no roots
Jackpots to journalists' truths.

It is the truth, it is the lie,
Heavy and thin as air,
Travelling as fast as dark running from light
Through a single whisper's might.

It is the winter wind,
Unpleasant yet equivalent
To the secrets vowed to never be uttered,
History that never met the ink cluttered.

Companies and families fall to its hand
It strikes everything like raging storm, unplanned,
Leaving even the king himself, shivering and scared!
It is the blackmail, the suicide, and the homicide bared.

I am no truth nor bluffs
But a whisper of destructions.

41. Death Note

Ever been lost, tried to find your way
But got more lost, deeper every day?
Looked side to side for clues in vain
But failed to reminisce, everything seemed blur
Lost in the screams and pain.

I tried to visualise and trace my steps back,
But the memory was black, a blank attack,
With only one white file to draw,
Highlighted 'TRUTH!' in red
That slowly dropped and fell to nothing.

I drew the file and saw my true path
Wrapped down by my tongue, aftermath.
I drew the file and saw my lies, unfold.
Backstabbing my friends to the bone, stories retold-
Dragging them by their feet to execution's cold.

I lied, and tears dropped, and bloodshed.
The knife held with words instead.
Thought my conscience was pure, white.
But blinded by power and gold.

A tainted soul to inherit hell

KATLEGO MASEMOLA

A soul more evil to send the Devil to retirement's bell.
My devious ways are now cunning me,
Unable to escape a mere guilt, how can it be?

Truth bottled, a ticking bomb,
I am sorry I cannot say 'I am sorry',
I cannot face anymore in this state,
Pills seem the way out, a sad fate.

42. Death Came

In courage and hope we choose to live
Thinking past today, more to give.
Plotting for tomorrow's light
Confident we'll be alright.
Showing no fear of death's call
Until he himself arrives to make us fall.

Quarter before six, an alarm's sound,
For the seventh time, echoes around.
Had to be up and ready at dawn,
The sun sneaks through the blinds, a new day's drawn,
Exposing the snake before the door,
Circling there, a silent roar.

The coward tried to leap,
But the bravery, a promise to keep,
I slowly rose from the bed's embrace,
With the aim of finding something to hit it with, steady
pace.
Only to trip, and before it I fell.
A moment's terror, life's tale to tell.

There I was, with it on the floor
Glaring straight into its eyes,

KATLEGO MASEMOLA

Mine wide and sore.
As if in a movie, life flashed by.
Body drenched in sweat, a moment stashed.
Is this my end?

INFINITE THOUGHTS

It gives me joy to know that you've made it this far.

KATLEGO MASEMOLA

The following is a bonus to read and enjoy.
Written in my native tongue.
Best regards...

43. Mahlale a ngwana

Ge e le go kgotla semana ka sa mafuri re kgotlile,
Re dira kgotla o mone re lebetše gore le a sobela.

Bo hlogo šweu ba lekile go lahlela a mabedi a mararo
Kgane ba tšhela letlapa ka meetse,
Thari ya hloka tsebe e le ga e dira tša mmapelo.
Di be di tsena di etšwa boka dipudi tša go hloka modiši.

Re be re itirile bo mahloadibona
Tsebo e falala boka noka e tswala.
Ga e le leleme be le dira mošomo wa lona,
Le eletša maaka, lenyatšo le boradia.

Mebila bošego be re e buša
Re itirile tšona tša bošego bo Lesilo Rula.
Re iphile boganka le bosenyi,
Dinotagi le diokobatši e le magobe a rena a mehla.

Ba lekile go re eletša
Eupša ra kgafa mantšu a bona
Lehono šita e šitile
Gago sana le go boela morago.

Lehono tša bošego di fihletše rena,

KATLEGO MASEMOLA

Ke rena bo Tsodio ga go sa robalega.
Re hlanola direthe re hlanolela lefela
Re boifa lege le fiša khirikhiri.

Thakgithakgi e a ithakgela
Tshinyitshinyi e a itshenyetša.
Ruri mahlale a ngwana a ka maragong
Ge a kgonana a tšhologa.

Di retwa ge di bowa mokatong
Rena re iphihlile re kota ke hlong

About the author

Katlego Makgwethe Masemola is a talented writer and storyteller, creative entrepreneur, and media expert. Born on March 20, 2001, in a village of Ga-Masemola in Limpopo, South Africa.

Katlego draws inspiration from the beauty of life and the depth of human emotions. His work explores themes of love, loss, and reliance, capturing the essence of the human experience with eloquence and grace. His upbringing has deeply influenced his perspective and approach to storytelling.

He holds a Bachelor of Arts in Creative Writing from the University of South Africa, Katlego Brings a wealth of knowledge and expertise to his craft. As a director of Fishermen JNK media house, he oversees a range of innovative projects, from content creating to media production.

Katlego also runs a popular YouTube channel called Fishermen JNK, where he and his crew shares insights and expertise with a growing audience. With specialisation to editing and proofreading, *he is dedicated to helping other refine their writing and communication skills.*

A natural leader, Katlego was a peer mentor at his school, Masemola Senior Secondary School, demonstrating his passion for empowering and inspiring others from an early age. Through his work, he aims to inspire and empower other to tell stories and share their ideas with the world.

In addition to writing Katlego enjoys reading, chess, and sports in general, which influences the vivid imagery and evident metaphors in his poems. When not writing, Katlego can be found playing sports or shooting videos for Fishermen JNK YouTube channel. He is always seeking new experiences and stories to tell.

You can directly communicate with the Katlego on FACEBOOK, Masemola Katlego or contact Fishermen JNK (PTY) Ltd to get contact.

INFINITE THOUGHTS

| KATLEGO M MASEMOLA